Dear Parent:
Your child's love of reading starts here!

Every child learns to read in a different way and at his or her own speed. Some go back and forth between reading levels and read favorite books again and again. Others read through each level in order. You can help your young reader improve and become more confident by encouraging his or her own interests and abilities. From books your child reads with you to the first books he or she reads alone, there are I Can Read Books for every stage of reading:

SHARED READING
Basic language, word repetition, and whimsical illustrations, ideal for sharing with your emergent reader

BEGINNING READING
Short sentences, familiar words, and simple concepts for children eager to read on their own

READING WITH HELP
Engaging stories, longer sentences, and language play for developing readers

READING ALONE
Complex plots, challenging vocabulary, and high-interest topics for the independent reader

ADVANCED READING
Short paragraphs, chapters, and exciting themes for the perfect bridge to chapter books

I Can Read Books have introduced children to the joy of reading since 1957. Featuring award-winning authors and illustrators and a fabulous cast of beloved characters, I Can Read Books set the standard for beginning readers.

A lifetime of discovery begins with the magical words "I Can Read!"

Visit www.icanread.com for information
on enriching your child's reading experience.

To Anita Bistrin and the cool kids of
Radcliff Elementary
—B.H.

For Sam, Nina, Levi, and Cree
—G.F.

I Can Read Book® is a trademark of HarperCollins Publishers.

Library of Congress Control Number: 2015947485
ISBN 978-0-06-227911-8 (trade bdg.) — ISBN 978-0-06-227910-1 (pbk.)

Typography by Victor Joseph Ochoa

16 17 18 19 20 SCP 10 9 8 7 6 5 4 3 2 1 ❖ First Edition

I Can Read!™

BEGINNING
1
READING

CLARK THE SHARK
LOST AND FOUND

WRITTEN BY **BRUCE HALE**   ILLUSTRATED BY **GUY FRANCIS**

"I have an exciting announcement," said Mrs. Inkydink to Clark's class. "Today is our field trip to the farmers' market!"

"Woo-hoo!" cried the class.

"WOO-HOO!" cried Clark the Shark.

"I've never seen a farmers' market."

"Please remember three things,"
said Mrs. Inkydink.
"Hold hands with your buddies,
follow instructions,
and use your inside voices."

Clark was so busy talking to Joey,
he wasn't paying attention.

"Did everyone get that?"
asked Mrs. Inkydink.

"Yes, teacher," said the class.

"Get what?" asked Joey.

8

"I don't know," said Clark.

"Hurrah-hooray, it's time to play!"

The farmers' market was exciting!
So much to see, so much to do,
and so much to eat.

"Look at all the FOOD!" cried Clark.

"Yum-yum-YUM!"

"What are the three things
Mrs. Inkydink told us
to remember?" asked Joey.

"Um, stick with your buddy,
don't get muddy, and, uh. . . .
I forget," said Clark.

"Hurrah-hooray, it's time to play!"
Clark and Joey tried the samples,
and Clark ate WAY too many!

They watched the jugglers,
but Clark didn't just watch.

When Clark heard some fun music,
he danced his funky shark dance.
But things got a little TOO funky!

By the time Clark and Joey

helped clean everything up,

their class was out of sight.

But Clark didn't want to go yet.

"Just one more song!" he said.

A big crowd was enjoying the music, and the two buddies got separated. "Joey?" said Clark. "Where are you?"

Clark looked under
the sea-grape stand,
but Joey wasn't there.

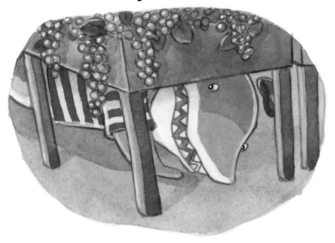

He looked by the jugglers,
but Joey wasn't there either.

Clark had lost his buddy and his class.

Clark was so worried

he couldn't eat, play, or hurrah-hooray.

"Maybe the three things
teacher told us to do will help,"
said Clark.
But what were they?

"Um, stay with your friend,
don't try to bend, and, uh. . . .
That's not it."

Clark bit his lip.

He wished he'd followed instructions, stuck with his buddy, and—

"That's it!" cried Clark.

"HEY, JOEY!" Clark yelled.

"I remember now. It's . . .

HOLD HANDS WITH YOUR BUDDIES,

FOLLOW INSTRUCTIONS,

AND USE YOUR INSIDE, um, voices?"

Clark shouted so loudly

that Joey came and found him.

And Joey wasn't the only one. . . .

"There you are!" said Mrs. Inkydink.

"I see I need to add a fourth rule."

"What's that?" asked Clark.

"If you ever get lost,"

said Mrs. Inkydink,

"stay in one spot and yell a lot!"

"That's one rule I can remember,"
said Clark the Shark.

CLARK THE SHARK'S BITE-SIZED FACTS

1 Sharks eat only when they're hungry, and sometimes days or even weeks pass between meals for big sharks.

2 Sharks don't have tongues! Their taste buds are in their throats and mouths.

3 Sharks are near the top of the food chain. This means that there is almost nothing in the sea that eats sharks.